HIV AROUND ME

Renee' Y. Burgess-Benson

HIV Around Me

Copyright © 2017 Renee' Y. Burgess-Benson

ISBN 9781521962169

Printed in USA by Amazon

Dedication

This book is dedicated to YOU! It's for every teenager and young adult reading this book. Education is the key to success and knowledge is and will always be powerful!

Table of Contents

Introduction 5

Middle School

My Nana 6

That Day with Dad 17

High School

Peer Pressure 29

My Best friend Jasmine 37

Resources

Introduction

I can sit here and give a million reasons why writing this book was necessary. I won't do that. I will tell you this. The statistics speak for themselves. Our Teens and Young Adults along with the 50 and up club are among the highest cases of newly diagnosed HIV infections in the US.

Through speaking with many teens and young adults I have found that most can care less about the numbers and reading articles. What they will do is be intrigued by a story that could very well be their own story, a story that hit so close to home that they share it with a peer, a story that makes them say they want to remain abstinent.

So I present to you 4 stories of HIV that could be anyone's story.

My Nana

Today was a half of school day and my nana picked me up. She told me that we had to make a few stops before we got home and I was ok with that as long as I got some food. I was hungry because we eat lunch so early and today we had meatloaf and it's so nasty that I knew I wasn't going to eat it. I can just taste the chicken nuggets from McDonald's before we even got there.

We pulled up to what looked like a doctor's office and the parking lot was full. People were coming in and out, some looking sad and others looking ok. I had never been here with nana and my curiosity was killing me to know what this place was. She told me I could take my food inside to finish eating. I sat down as she went to sign in and while I was waiting for her to come back to her seat I overheard this man and lady talking. She was upset about something that he did and she told him that if the doctor told her anything other than the truth she would be angry. She cursed at him and even said if the outcome wasn't what she wanted she was leaving him.

Nana came and sat by me and asked if I was ok and I told her I was. I started looking around while waiting and noticed a stand with a lot of pamphlets on them. Most of them were talking about something called HIV and how people needed to get tested. Now my mind was stuck on this HIV stuff. What was it and what did it have to do with my nana? I wanted to ask her so bad but I didn't want her to think I was being nosey and all she'd do is tell me to say in a child's place and it's none of my business.

A nurse came out and called a name. The couple that was arguing got up and went in the back. I'm still sitting here wondering what

HIV is so I lean over and whisper to my nana and ask her. Just as I figured she gave me this look that she gives when I'm being nosey. A few minutes go by and the nurse comes out again and this time she calls my nana's name. I figured she was going to tell me to sit here and wait for her to come out but she didn't she said, "Come on child, let's go!" Here I was about to go behind the scenes of what? I have no idea.

We get in the back and the nurse asks my nana to stand on the scale. Man I had no idea that my nana was 168 pounds. I'm only, wait I don't even know. I asked the nurse could I see what my weight was and she said I could. I got on the scale and it said 98 pounds. I was almost 100 pounds and that was exciting to me because for most of my life I've been the skinny kid. Well I still am because all my friends are still bigger than me. The nurse then asks nana to sit in this chair next to the blood pressure machine and she takes her temperature. So far so good with my nana and we walk behind the nurse down this hallway. It looked so long and we went to the last room on the left, Room 7.

The nurse told my nana to have a seat by the desk where the doctor would sit and I sat in the chair next to her. She started asking all these questions to my nana and she was answering them. I wasn't really paying attention but then I heard the nurse ask her if she was taking her medicine as prescribed. I looked up and over at my nana and was in shock because I never knew nana was taking any medicine. My nana was a tall woman with long sandy red hair, freckles, and average sized in weight. I had never once seen my nana take medicine and always thought to myself that she was one of the healthiest people I knew. She always knows the remedy for anything someone is feeling. I was now wondering what kind of medicine my nana was taking and for what.

Just as I started back eating my food there was a knock at the door and the doctor came in. He shook my hand and shook my nana's and sat on this stool at the desk. He started logging into the computer and pulled up something and gave my nana this look. He then said to her, "are you taking your medicine everyday?" She responded to him that she tries to take it every day but it's become hard and that she often thinks about how she has to take this medicine for the rest of her life. Now my mom and nana always tell me to mind my business but I am sitting here confused. What medicine for the rest of your life? Before I knew it I had blurted out, "What is going on Nana? What is wrong with you and why are you taking medicine for the rest of your life?" She looked at the doctor and he looked at me and then said to her that she needed to just go ahead and do what she planned to do at this visit. Little did I know she was about to tell me news that would change my life.

My nana looked over at me with a look in her eyes of worry. I had never seen this look from her before and as I was looking in her eyes she started talking. She started saying that the medicine she was taking and will take the rest of her life was for a disease called HIV. The doctor asked me if I knew what HIV was and I explained to him that I had heard of it before when people were talking about that Tyler Perry Movie called Temptation. My nana then told me that she has had it for years before I was ever born. Then I was asked if I knew what HIV stood for, which I didn't. The doctor pulled out this tablet that had all of these pictures of what looked like blood cells and pills and paragraphs and paragraphs of words.

The doctor asked me if anything looks familiar to me. I told him I wasn't quite sure so he said that he would explain to me what HIV and AIDS were. He started by telling me that HIV is a virus that attacks your blood cells the cells that help fight infection sometimes they're called T helper cells. HIV stands for human immunodeficiency virus and AIDS stands for acquired immune deficiency syndrome. He also told me that HIV is spread many ways. You can get HIV from having unprotected sex, sometimes people get it from blood transfusions, babies can get it from their moms, and blood-to-blood contact. Everything the doctors told me sounded so crazy I could not imagine my Nana getting HIV for any of these ways. My mind was so curious I just had to ask my Nana which one of these happened to her. My Nana told me that after her and my mom's dad divorced she met a man who she thought was going to be the man that she would probably spend the rest of her life with. She said that because they talked about everything in life from past, present, and what they want in the future she thought she knew everything about him until one day she watched him get really sick, so sick that he had to go to the hospital. When my Nana went to go and visit they told her that if she went in the room she had to put on a gown because they didn't know what was wrong and didn't want anybody else to get sick.

At this point I look over my Nana and she's crying. I look at the doctor and the doctor is crying. My Nana continued the story; she then tells us that the doctor asked her if she had been tested for this new disease that was spreading like wildfire. She said no and the doctor said let's test you now and when she got tested it came back saying that she had AIDS. Now at this point I know I'm only in middle school but I'm trying to understand. My Nana just told me that she had HIV and now she's saying that the doctor told her when she was tested that she had AIDS. So of course here is my curiosity again asking my Nana questions. I didn't want to bug my Nana anymore so I looked at the doctor and I asked, "How does Nana now have HIV but when she first got her test done they said she had AIDS?" I think everybody in the world should be glad we have doctors because it seems like they have all the answers to all of our questions no matter what it is. My Nana's doctor told me that when my Nana was first told of her sickness that all they knew was AIDS and it wasn't until years later that they knew that there was such a thing as HIV before AIDS. Well that makes a lot of sense I'm starting to understand this whole HIV and AIDS talk.

Now that I understood what HIV and AIDS meant and the difference between the two the doctor showed me a diagram. The caption on the diagram said that it was the HIV virus attacking cells in the body to take them over and to make more copies of itself, this is what HIV does it attacks the body, it tries to make you weak. The doctor saying that every time my Nana comes in for a visit they take her blood and it's sent to lab and a test that they do with the blood lets the doctors know what medicines my Nana can take and what she can't. It also lets the doctor know if the one she is taking is working at fighting the HIV. The ones she can take are the ones that keep her alive and they keep the HIV virus from attacking her.

Getting out of school early today sure has been one adventure. I would say that getting my McDonalds was a highlight of my day but it wasn't the best part of my day was knowing that my Nana its okay and that even if she does have this HIV virus it doesn't change the fact that she's my Nana and that I love her the same. My Nana said that she was going to take me to the library so I can find some books that talk a lot more about HIV and AIDS so that as I get older and I understand more I will know exactly what to do as a teenager and adult to protect myself and those around me from anything that can hurt them. I can't wait to go back with my Nana to the doctor again so that I can ask this doctor a lot more questions because I know once I start reading and I don't put the book down and my curiosity gets the best of me I'm going to want an answer and I just know he's going to have every answer I need.

That Day with Dad

My dad has always been the kind of guy who had a lot of friends. Lately I noticed he wasn't hanging out as much and had become distant from my uncles. Well not my real uncles but I called them uncle because they were like brothers to my dad and they had known each other since they were my age, 13. I didn't think to ask my dad where they were because sometimes they'd get into a disagreement and not speak for days or weeks. Here it was almost 5 months and not one word or conversation of them. Still I just chalked it up as them being mad at each other.

I usually spent time at school during lunch with my friend Josh who is my dad's friend JJ Sr.'s son. Today when I went to sit by Josh he told me that he couldn't be my friend anymore and that I had to find someone else to be with during lunch time. This pissed me off and I asked him why and what if anything did I do to him? He ignored me and walked away. I didn't know what to think but this was my best friend and for him to just cut me off like that was crazy.

I'm in this math class trying to concentrate on a new technique the teacher is giving but my mind won't stop racing. What in the world did I do to Josh? Was I talking to a girl he liked? Did I take something that I didn't know was his? Did I forget to do something I promised? My mind raced until the bell rang. I couldn't even tell you what the teacher talked about today. I had one more class left and then school was out. I needed to get home soon so that I can ask my dad if he knew what was going on.

So glad to finally be home, I got off the bus and ran through the house straight to my dad. I yelled to him as I made my way to the back of the house in the den area where he was watching TV. I started telling him how I noticed that he and Uncle JJ hasn't spoke in almost 5 months and that when I got to school today and saw Josh in lunch he told me that we couldn't speak or be friend anymore. My dad sat up so fast in his recliner chair that I thought he broke it. He was like what do you mean you can't be friends with Josh anymore? I explained to him that when I asked Josh why he never gave me a reason and walked off. My dad then got up and was pacing the floor and mumbling under his breath. I could have sworn I heard a curse word or two but nonetheless he was angry.

I left out the den and went to put my books in my room but all of a sudden I heard this loud yelling. I peeped around the corner into the kitchen and I saw him on the phone. He was talking to JJ and he was yelling at him saying that the kids had nothing to do with them and that he was wrong for telling Josh he couldn't be friends with me anymore. They were on the phone almost 15 minutes going back and forth and cursing. Next thing I know is I heard my dad say that he didn't have anything else to say unless it was face to face and that he and I were going to their house. Come on dad really? That's all I could say to myself. Why is my dad making things harder for me at school by making me go to Josh's house? He chose to not be my friend anymore and frankly I'm ok with that. It's not even a big deal, but to my dad it was huge.

We only stayed about 20 minutes from Uncle JJ and Josh but we got there in almost 10 minutes. My dad had me so scared he was swerving and talking and talking and swerving. Now I have seen my dad angry but this was a new level of anger I never knew he could be. We pulled up to Uncle JJ's house and he and Josh came out the house before we could get out the car good. He was yelling at my dad to leave and my dad said no we weren't leaving until we settled this once and for all. In my mind, I'm thinking what does he mean settle this? Settle what? I had never seen my Uncle Josh and my dad so mad at each other and neither did Josh. We ended up standing next to each other both in fear because our dad's got so close we thought they were about to start fighting.

I grabbed Josh just as he was about to try and break our dad's up and then I heard Uncle JJ yell out to Josh and say, "Don't you grab my son! You might have AIDS just like you're nasty daddy!" You know how you do a double take look? Well that's what I did! I moved my arm from in front of Josh and I stood there in shock. At this point the neighbors and my dad's other friend who was in Uncle JJ's house were outside watching in case a fight broke out. When he yelled that out everything got silent. My dad looked at me and demanded that I get in the car. All I could do was get in the car.

Once we got in the car I started asking my dad what was going on and why did Uncle JJ say he had AIDS? My dad looked over at me and said that we would talk about it when we got home. That had to be the longest 20-minute ride home I had ever experienced in my life. There was no music, no talking, and no breathing so it seems. It was so quiet that I could hear my stomach growling. I didn't eat lunch today because I was so upset that Josh stopped being my friend so I just went to the library and read some books.

Before we got home my dad stopped to the gas station to fill up his tank. While he was inside paying for gas my nose started running so I was fumbling around looking for tissues. I didn't see any in the usual places so I figured I would check the glove compartment box. When I opened it I found tissues but I also found a pill bottle. Why did my dad have a pill bottle in his car? He was coming out to pump the gas so I quickly read the medicine name on the bottle and closed it real fast. When we got home my dad told me to go in my room, start on my homework, and that he would get me food to eat soon. While I was in my room I could hear him through the walls in his room talking to someone on the phone. I heard him say that Uncle JJ had blurted out that he had AIDS and that he needed to tell me but he didn't know how to tell me.

Tell me what? I know I am only 13 but I needed answers. So I went to my dad's door and asked him if we could talk. He yelled at me and said no! So I said to him, "What is Atripla for?" There was silence and then I heard him say, "Let me call you back". Today must be the day for silence because boy I tell you he was silent for almost a minute. Next thing I know is I heard his doorknob turn and he opened the door. His eyes were red as if he had been crying. "Come with me", he said as we walked over to the dining room table in the kitchen. He begins to explain how he knows so much happened today and he was going to tell me everything I needed to know right now.

He started telling me about my mom and how I was too young to remember but when I was 3 years old my mom got very sick. She was put in the hospital and within a week she died. I knew this story because growing up I always asked where my mommy was and my dad and grandma always told me that God came down and took her to be his angel. Well what my dad didn't tell me and is now telling me is that my mom had AIDS. My mom died from AIDS and that she found out that she had it that day she got admitted into the hospital August 5, 1986. Now I was in tears. My mom found out on my birthday and sitting here I can barely remember seeing a glimpse of her lying in this bed with tubes everywhere taking her hand and wiping a tear from my eye. That was the last time I saw my mom alive.

All of these questions started to come to my mind. I knew a little about HIV and AIDS like how it was transmitted in many ways like unprotected sex and drugs but how did my mom get it? So I asked my dad. His response shocked me.

My dad told me that before I was born he and my mom broke up and she began seeing this man who said he'd give her the world. He claimed he could give her all the things I couldn't give her. What he didn't do is tell her that he was infected with HIV and that my mom wouldn't be the first woman he has given it to. After I was born my mom wanted us to be a family so she went back to my dad so that I didn't grow up without him in my life. Still not knowing that she was infected her and my dad had sex multiple times and she even got pregnant again but had a miscarriage before she had a chance to see the doctor.

Those three years went by and she got sicker and sicker as the days went on to eventually she thought she had the flu. She went to the doctor and he gave her medicines to get rid of the flu he thought she had but nothing was working. The day she went to the hospital her fever was 104.5 and she couldn't walk and could barely speak. They ran all the tests you could think of and eventually one of the doctors suggested running the test for AIDS. So many people in the last few years had been diagnosed and died from this new disease that now when anyone got sick they added it to the list of tests to perform.

On my third birthday my mom was told she had AIDS, which at the time is what they called it. My dad asked me if I was ready to know why Uncle JJ said what he said. Well why not? I think I already know that he's probably got it too. From everything I have learned in health class I'm sure my mom and dad had unprotected sex and she gave my dad AIDS too.

My guess was correct. My dad said that the same day she found out they requested that he be tested too and his test came back positive. So I asked him why Uncle JJ yelled that out in so much anger if he's had this disease now for almost 10 years. He said that Uncle JJ found those pills in his glove box one day while looking for the title to the car when

I was about to sell it to one of his friends who didn't believe I owned the car. Uncle JJ researched the pills and saw they were for people with HIV and he felt betrayed. My dad said that most people who are uneducated and don't understand have what's called Stigma. That wasn't a word I had ever heard before so I asked him what it meant. Stigma is when you discriminate against someone because of a condition he or she has that you don't understand.

Uncle JJ didn't know he was safe just being around my dad and because he knew my dad has HIV he assumed that I had it too. That explains why Josh can't be my friend or be around me anymore.

My dad explained to me that not everyone would understand what it's like to be HIV positive. This is why it's so important to educate yourself and others around you. On this day, with my dad, it's one I will never forget as long as I am alive.

Peer Pressure

"I don't care if I have known you since you were born you are wrong and you know it!" is what I told Matt when I found out he was behind all of the rumors and hatred going on towards one of our classmates. Matt and I grew up together since 5th grade and here we were in 10th grade and sophomores in high school. Why were we arguing?

Growing up I was always the star player for most sports; basketball, football, and baseball. Other students in the school looked up to me and valued what I thought around the school. One day we got a new student and he seemed very quiet and reserved. He would speak if spoken to but never initiated conversation. On this one particular day probably half way through the school year everyone started hearing rumors that he was gay and had HIV. Now me personally I don't care about all of that but I was the most popular kid in school. When others would say things degrading to him I would join in with the laughter and jokes.

Peer pressure is one of those things that you're warned about your whole school life but until you're faced with right and wrong choices you never really see it or deal with it. I chose to be a leader and in doing so I had others who saw me pick at the new kid and make fun of him all the time. One thing I never did was physically bother him. I didn't think it was right to do that but others did and that's what made me finally take a stand and speak up!

I will never forget this day as long as I live. It was homecoming/spirit week and each day of the week we had to dress up as different characters. Monday was Hobo Day, Tuesday was Crazy Sock Day, Wednesday was Wild and Wacky Day, Thursday was Throwback Thursday, and Friday was Freestyle Friday. This time was the most exciting time of the school year! Well for some of us. On that Monday everyone was dressed as bums and having fun taking pictures and making fun of each other. It was lunchtime and I was starving so as soon as the bell rang I made my way over to the cafeteria. As I was walking through the food court I noticed a crowd that grew as more people came out of class for lunch. I got closer and noticed in the middle of the circle was the new guy. He was just standing there looking and gripping his books. His backpack was on his shoulders and he looked like a bum.

The sad part is that he dressed like that every day. Classmates were yelling out at him saying how he was dirty and he was the winner of the Hobo Day Award. I then noticed out of the corner of my eye someone launching a rock at him. The rock hit him on the side of his head just above his left eyebrow. He grabbed his face and fell to the ground. Blood was coming out and one of our female classmates was about to run up to him and help when Matt yelled out, "Don't touch him he's got AIDS!" Now at the time I didn't know if it was true or not it was just a rumor but everyone screamed and ran. I even heard someone yell for the school nurse.

As the school nurse helped him up off the ground some were still watching and mumbling about what Matt yelled out and asking each other if it was true. Did he have AIDS? The next day in Science class we all entered as usual but when the new guy came in everyone who sat near or next to him moved their desk. This seemed odd to the teacher who has no idea what was going on so he asked, "What seems to be the problem? Why are you moving those desks around?" Jennifer, the same girl who was about to help the new guy yesterday said to Mr. Brokowski that the new kid had AIDS and everyone was afraid they would get it. Little did we know the lesson on HIV and AIDS was about to begin. Besides this was a science class.

"Well class, take your seats. We haven't even got to the chapter in our books on infectious diseases but who says we have to go in order? You think that HIV and AIDS is that easy to catch?" the whole class answered yes. "What if I told you that you can't get HIV or AIDS from sweat, hugs, tears, saliva, or touching?" Everyone in the class was silent. I was watching the expressions on everyone's face. Jennifer raised her hand and asked, "So it's not airborne?" "Oh heavens no!" answered Mr. Brokowski. "HIV and AIDS is one of those things that you can't even see outside the body. You can't look at someone and tell that they even have it. So to assume that a classmate or anyone has it would be just that, an assumption. HIV and AIDS have no race, gender, age, or preference on which it infects. So the next time you think that someone might have it you might want to think again because you will have no idea".

The bell rang for us to change classes but before everyone had a chance to get up and leave I stood up and asked Mr. Brokowski if I could say something. I knew that many people looked up to me and that if I didn't say something it would almost be as if I condoned being a bully and harassing the new student. I looked over to the new guy and I said to him, "On behalf of my peers I want to extend an apology. Not just for what was assumed but also for the actions taken. I was not raised to be a bully or to think that I was better than anyone else. Sadly I allowed the pressures of my peers and the pressures to remain popular among them get in the way of my integrity and what I know is the right thing to do. Whether you have HIV or not that's not my place or anyone else's place to judge you. So for all that you have endured I am sorry". I walked to him and gave him a handshake and to my surprise everyone in the class apologized and the circle of hate that surrounded him the day before was now a circle of love.

On this day I realized that the new guy could have been me. I could have been picked on, hit with rocks, and make the laughing stock of the school. How you might ask? Because although I was the star Football player, Basketball player, and one of the most popular kids in the school. I am also someone who was born HIV Positive.

My Best Friend Jasmine

Since she was two and I was four Jasmine and I have been friends. In fact she is my best friend in the whole world! Growing up together in church was fun. I know we were supposed to paying attention in church but we couldn't help but pass notes back and forth on the church bulletin. We'd play tic-tac-toe, hangman, or just talk about stuff. Jasmine went to one school and I went to another but that didn't stop us from sleeping over each other's house every weekend.

Here we are now 11 and 13 and who knew I would one day be saving her life. I can remember it like it was yesterday. We used to love riding our bikes around the neighborhood. Our destination was usually either the park at the elementary school or to Taco Bell. We loved that place and saved money every weekend so we could eat there.

The Taco Bell was on the other side of a busy intersection and wasn't close to the crosswalk. We hated having to go way down the street just to cross and ride all the way back down so when no traffic was coming we'd dart as fast as we can across the street. Now I will admit I was no pro riding that bike at all. I was still scared to ride the bike off the curb.

On the Saturday that Taco Bell had tacos buy one get one free we were so ready! We woke up just in time for lunch, got a shower, and got on our bikes. There was this very large hill on Jasmine's street that everyone had fun going down but hated going up. Everything that day seemed so right. I went down that hill super fast and I said that day I'd be a daredevil and go down without holding the handlebars. I did it! Man that was the scariest thing I had ever done and I didn't fall off my bike! I was so winning that day!

Jasmine and I got to the spot where we crossed with our bikes to go to Taco Bell and usually I go first and she follows to make sure I get my bike up and down the curb. Out of nowhere Jasmine darted past me and went out into the street. She got to the median and as she went to ride off the other side of the median she crashed. She fell off her bike and was lying in the middle of the road. I panicked! All I could do was rush to her. She was bleeding from her arm where she got a huge scrape from hitting the concrete. As I got to her I went to put my bike down to the ground it went the opposite direction and the chain ring ripped a huge piece of skin off my hand. I was so worried about Jasmine that I didn't even think about all the blood on either of us. I grabbed her up took my jacket off and was trying to tie it around her arm. It was bleeding badly.

Traffic came to a halt and a guy stopped his car to help us to the sidewalk. I was able to run inside Taco Bell and gave the manager the number to call for Jasmine's mom to come. When she got there she rushed us to the ER. My mom was on the way but I couldn't help but notice all of the panic. All she did was fall off her bike and get a little scrape on her arm. Why were the doctors asking so many questions? My mom got there and she was in the hallway talking to Jasmine's mom. All of a sudden I saw my mom grab her face like she was crying. She looked through my room window and then turned back to talk to Jasmine's mom.

My mom finally came in my room and I asked her why she was crying and what in the world was going on. That's when she told me something that would change my life forever. Jasmine was HIV positive and when I helped her get off the ground my blood and open wound came in contact with hers and they will have to do months of testing to know if it passed to me. I sat there in shock. I knew what HIV and AIDS was because the school I went to was a medical based program school so we talked about everything you can think of in the medical field. I was terrified but then I began to get angry. I asked my mom how she could allow me to be around Jasmine knowing that she had HIV and had it ever since she got sick as a child and needed a blood transfusion. My mom said that she didn't want me or anyone else to treat Jasmine different so she wasn't going to tell me until I was older and hoped nothing happened like this to make her have to tell me sooner.

I wasn't so mad anymore but I was still scared. What if I had HIV? People would find out and treat both of us bad. The doctor said I had to come back to be tested in 3 months and at 6 months after I had been exposed. In the first 3 months I still went to spend the weekends with Jasmine. We talked about how we both felt. She was afraid when she saw me rushing to her and said that she always did everything so safe to make sure she didn't get hurt around me. I told her it wasn't her fault and that she was and will always be my best friend and if I had to help her I would do it again.

It's now 3 months later and I was on the way to the clinic to be tested with my mom. I was afraid. My mom was afraid. Nobody wants to be told they have HIV. The doctors insisted that we do the two-week wait versus the quick test because of the severity of the situation. Both tests are equally accurate but they didn't want to take any risks. So I had to get stuck by a needle and have blood drawn out my arm. The hardest part was waiting two whole weeks.

The time has come. The results are in and today we will find out if I have HIV or not. The room was so cold and dull. How appropriate to put me in a room full of sad feelings. To make matters worse another doctor was going to be giving me my results and he came in looking like Lurch. He was tall so his white coat looked like a long gown on him. He walked slow and had a voice like that guy on the Clear Eyes Commercial. He sat down on the stool and logged into the computer. As he's talking I seem to drift away. I could hear him talking but everything was a blur. My mom nudged me and said, "Did you hear that? You're Negative!" Oh my God! I'm negative! I was overjoyed to hear those results.

I tested negative for HIV but my best friend Jasmine has to be positive her whole life. That doesn't change anything though. When we are old and gray with grandkids we will still be the best of friends. True friendship will defy the odds!

Resources for Teens about HIV

HIV Among Youth
http://www.cdc.gov/hiv/group/age/youth/
Being Young and Positive
http://www.avert.org/living-with-hiv/health-wellbeing/being-young-positive

Parents & Teachers

Information on Teens & HIV/AIDS
http://www.pamf.org/parenting-teens/sexuality/stds/hiv-aids/aids.html
Talking With Teens
http://www.hhs.gov/ash/oah/resources-and-publications/info/parents/just-facts/hiv-aids.html

Also Visit...
The Official Website for Renee Burgess-Benson
www.ladybyrdlive.com

The Official Website for the LadyByrd Live Foundation
www.ladybyrdlivefoundation.org

Made in the USA
Columbia, SC
19 May 2021